This book belongs to:

_____

For Jan and Paul

First published in Great Britain in 1988 by Andersen Press Ltd.,

20 Vauxhall Bridge Road, London SW1V 2SA.

This paperback edition first published in 2010 by Andersen Press Ltd.

Published in Australia by Random House Australia Pty.,

Level 3, 100 Pacific Highway, North Sydney, NSW 2060.

Copyright © Tony Ross, 1988

The rights of Tony Ross to be identified as the author and illustrator

of this work have been asserted by him in accordance with

the Copyright, Designs and Patents Act, 1988.

All rights reserved.

Colour separated in Switzerland by Photolitho AG, Zürich.

Printed and bound in Singapore by Tien Wah Press.

10   9   8   7   6   5   4   3   2   1

British Library Cataloguing in Publication Data available.

ISBN 978 1 84939 016 3

This book has been printed on acid-free paper

SUPER DOOPER
JEZEBEL

TONY ROSS

ANDERSEN PRESS

Jezebel was perfect in every way. She was so perfect,
she was called Super Dooper Jezebel.

When other children came out of school, they were sometimes untidy,

but Jezebel was always super dooper neat.

Jezebel always kept her room tidy, and she always
put her things back in their boxes . . .

and she cleaned up after the cat.

When she went out to play with her friends,

Jezebel always kept clean. (She still liked
to have two baths every day.)

She always wrote her "thank you" letters, in neat writing, without being reminded,

and at school, she was best at everything.

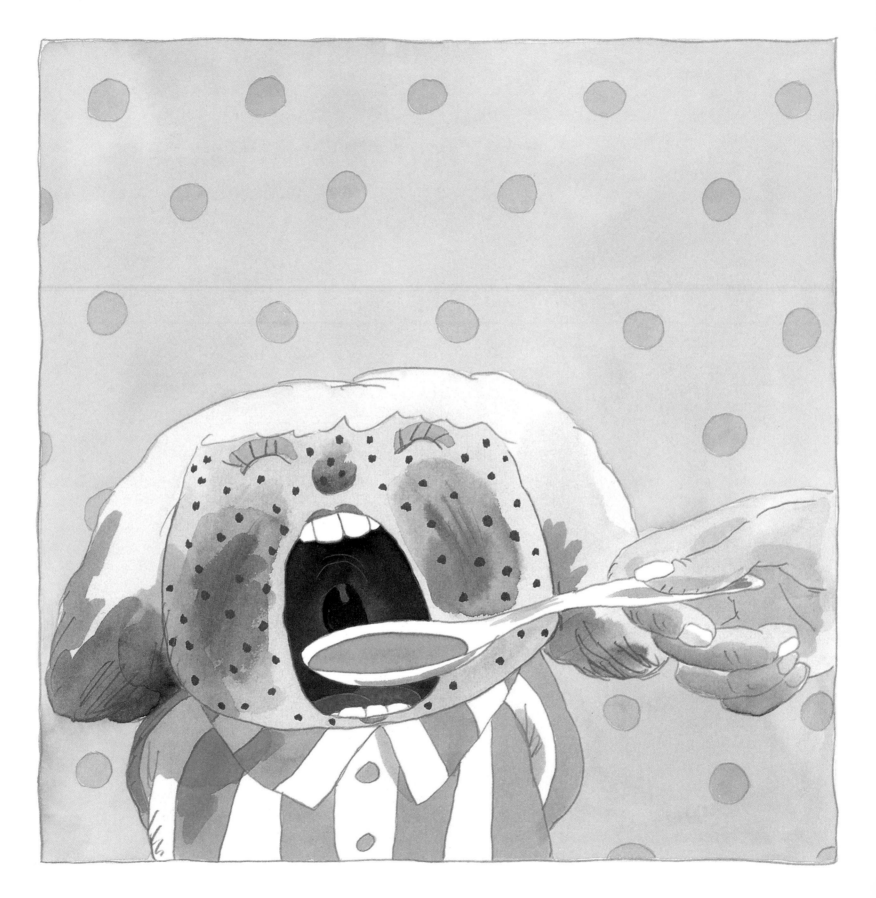

When she had spots, she always took her medicine
(and said, "Thank you").

She could do up buttons, and tie real bows on her lace-ups.

Jezebel always ate up her meals. She always
put her knife and fork together.

And she *never* picked her nose.

Jezebel told other children not to do things . . .

because it was nice being perfect.

When the Prime Minister heard about Jezebel,
she sent a special medal for being good,

and a special statue of Jezebel was put up in the park,
to remind everybody else to try to be perfect.

She even went on television, in a special show
to talk about herself and her medal,

and the cups she had won for being polite, being spotless, being helpful, being best at sums, reading, poetry and writing.

At school, Super Dooper Jezebel wouldn't do *anything* wrong . . .

like the other noisy children who weren't perfect . . .

CLUMP!

TONY ROSS

Tony Ross was born in London and trained at the Liverpool School of Art. He has worked as a cartoonist, graphic designer, and art director of an advertising agency. He is now considered to be one of the finest contemporary children's illustrators, and his books are published all over the world.

Tony Ross has illustrated over eight hundred books for children, many of which are considered modern classics. His books include: *Tadpole's Promise*, *I Hate School*, *Mayfly Day*, and *I'm Coming to Get You!*, as well as the bestselling Little Princess books, which have now been made into an award-winning animated television series.

Other books by Tony Ross:

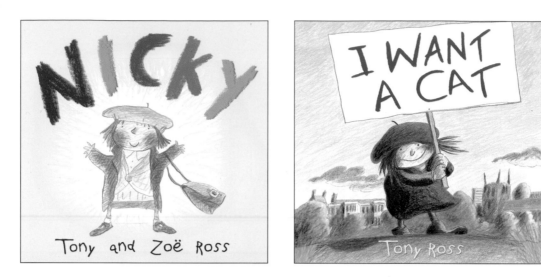

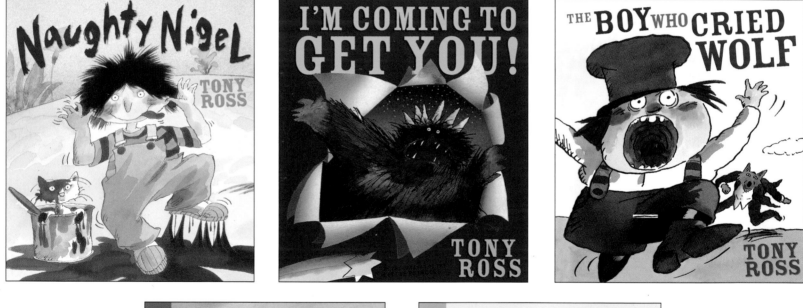

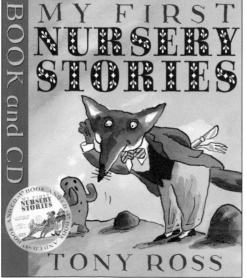

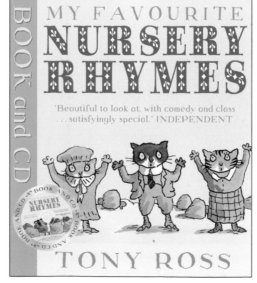